# EMMA'S TURN TO DANCE

**Written and illustrated by LOU ALPERT**

*Whispering Coyote Press Inc./New York*

To Lanham & Barbara Lyne

Special Thanks
To My Daughters
ANGIE & EMMA

Published by Whispering Coyote Press Inc.
P.O. Box 2159, Halesite, New York 11743-2159
Text copyright © 1991 by Lou Alpert
Illustrations copyright © 1991 by Lou Alpert
Printed in the United States of America
ISBN 1-879085-00-3

Emma is 4 years old. Her sister Angie is 12, and she is a dancer.

Angie leaps down the hall, twirls thru the house, and constantly looks at herself in every mirror.

Four times a week Mother drives Angie to dance class where she leaps, points and pliés with lots of other kids.

Once a year Angie gets to wear beautiful costumes and to dance on a big stage. This is called a DANCE RECITAL.

The whole family, including Angie's brothers, come to watch her
perform. Angie gets to wear make-up. Emma thinks her big sister
looks like a movie star.

At the end of the show Daddy always gives Angie one red rose!

Sometimes Angie lets Emma wear her old costumes and teaches Emma her dance steps.

They turn on music and dance thru the house. Angie says, "Emma you're very good, I think someday you'll be a dancer!"

At night when Emma sleeps, she dreams that she's the greatest dancer in the world. She leaps thru the clouds, twirls thru the air and shines so bright the stars turn away in wonder.

But when Emma wakes up she's still only 4 years old. Emma dreams of the day when it will be her turn to dance.

When Emma's cousin Amanda comes to play they pretend to be dance teachers.

Emma's favorite doll, Ginny, can even do an arabesque!

But when Amanda leaves, Emma is still just 4 years old. Emma
dreams of the day when it will be her turn to dance.

One day, Emma's mother came home with a special surprise. When Emma opened the box she found a pair of pink ballet slippers. She couldn't believe it!

"Emma, would you like to take dancing with Ms. Denise?" her mother asked. "YES! YES! YES!" cried Emma.

Every week Emma's mother took her to dance class. There were five other girls just Emma's size.

All the girls would put their arms over their heads, stretching and twisting back and forth like washing machines.

Ms. Denise would lay a lovely colored scarf on the floor. Each girl would leap over it. Ms. Denise called this "Over the Rainbow." Emma even learned to bow and curtsy.

One day Ms. Denise sat the class on the floor and said, "it's time to learn a special dance to do for our family and friends." Emma raised her hand and asked, "is this our dance recital?" Ms. Denise said "yes." Emma asked, "will we have costumes?" Ms. Denise showed them a picture of the most beautiful blue costume Emma had ever seen! Emma asked, "can we wear make-up?" Ms. Denise said, "that's up to your mothers."

The weeks flew by and soon it was the night before Emma's recital.
Everything was ready.

Emma was so excited she couldn't sleep. Her daddy came in and gave Emma a big hug. "You'll be the most wonderful dancer in the whole show," he said. Emma gave her daddy a kiss and went right to sleep.

The next afternoon Emma's whole family drove to her recital.

When they arrived, Emma's mother took her to the dressing room while the rest of the family went into the auditorium. She put Emma's hair in a bun and pinned in her hairpiece. Finally, she put lipstick on Emma.

After a kiss and a hug Emma's mother went to join the rest of her family.

As Emma looked at herself in the mirror, she felt butterflies in her stomach. She could hear the music begin for the first dancers.

Finally, it was time for Emma's class to perform. Emma danced out on the stage. She twirled to the music.

She did an arabesque, and SMILED!

Emma curtsied as her whole family stood up and cheered!

At the end of the show Emma's daddy gave her one red rose!

Emma is 4 years old. Emma is a DANCER!